SAXTON FREYMANN AND JOOST ELFFERS

HOW ARE YOU PEELING?
Foods with Moods

ARTHUR A. LEVINE BOOKS

AN IMPRINT OF SCHOLASTIC PRESS

NEW YORK

HOW ARE YOU

FEELING?

Happy?
Sad?

Feeling blue?
Feeling bad?

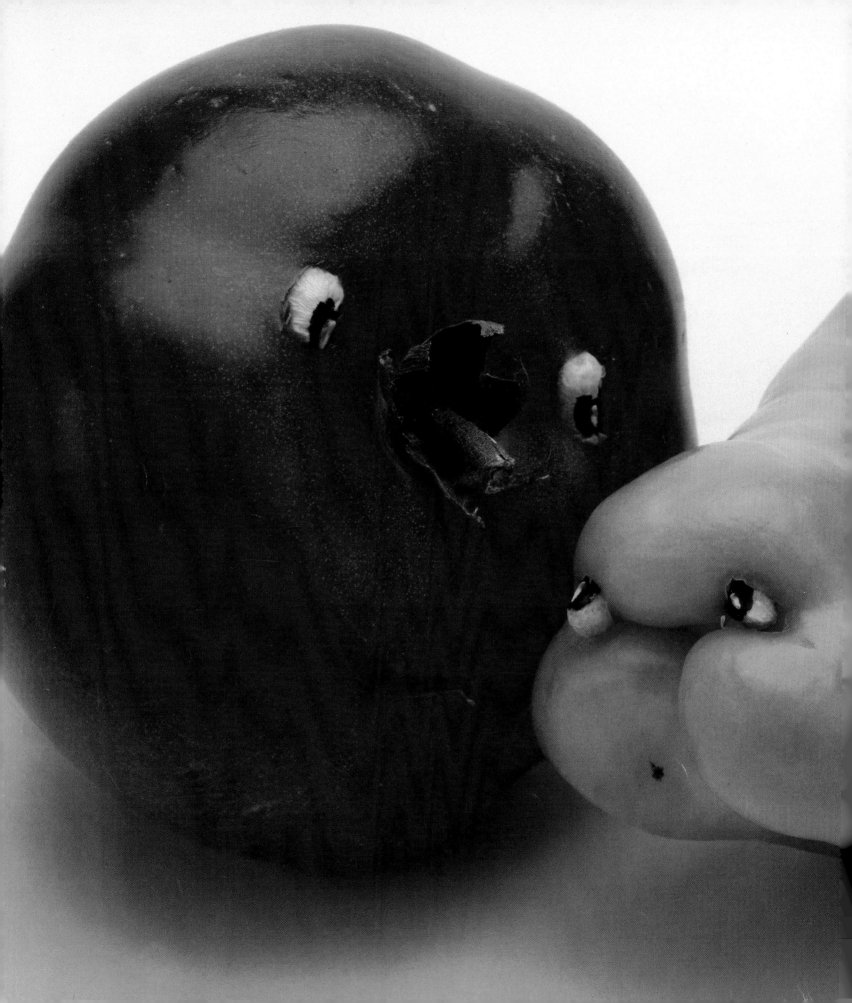

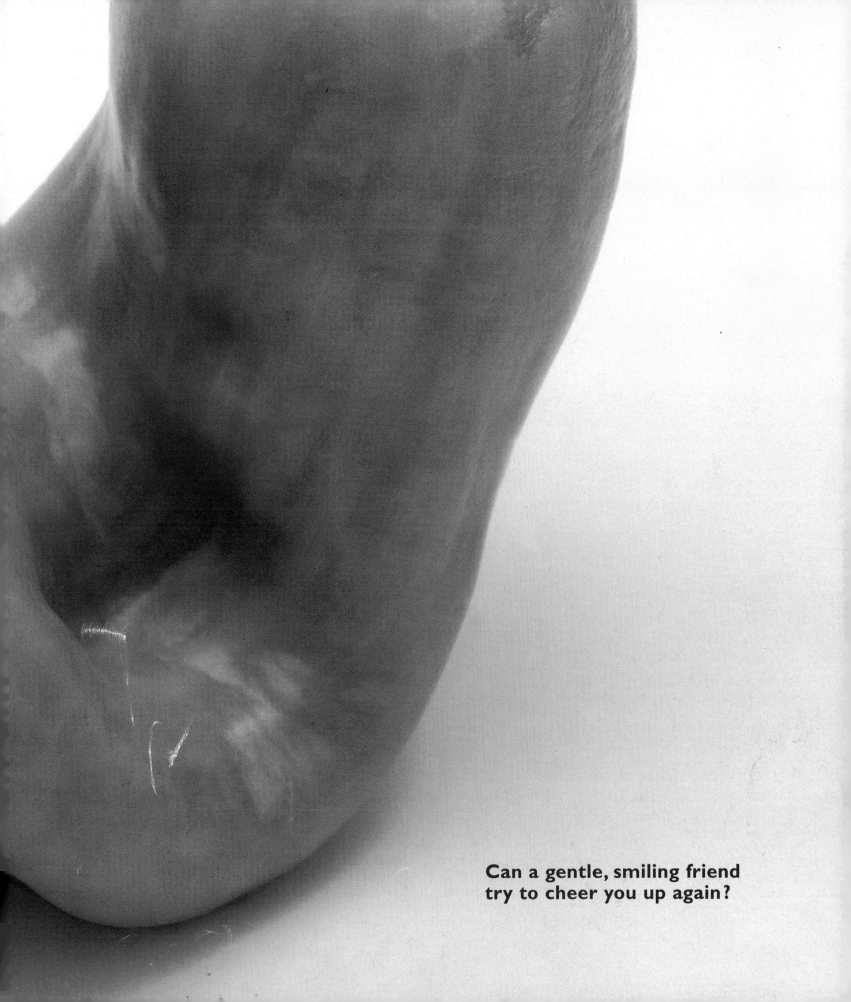

**Can a gentle, smiling friend
try to cheer you up again?**

When you have to wait, because someone is late,
are you bored? Jumpy? Worried? Grumpy?
Excited as the minutes pass?
Now your friend is here at last!

How are you when friends drop by?

With someone new...a little shy?

Don't belong?

Not for long!

Feel secure?

Or not so sure?

Amused?
Confused?
Frustrated?
Surprised?
Try these feelings
on for size.

HOW ARE

YOU FEELING?

When you're attacked, do you react?

How do you feel
when someone is mean?
Timid? Bold?
Or in-between?

When you're angry, do you pout? Whine? Cry? Scream? Shout?

Feeling sorry
and ashamed?
Or embarrassed
to be blamed?

Jealous?

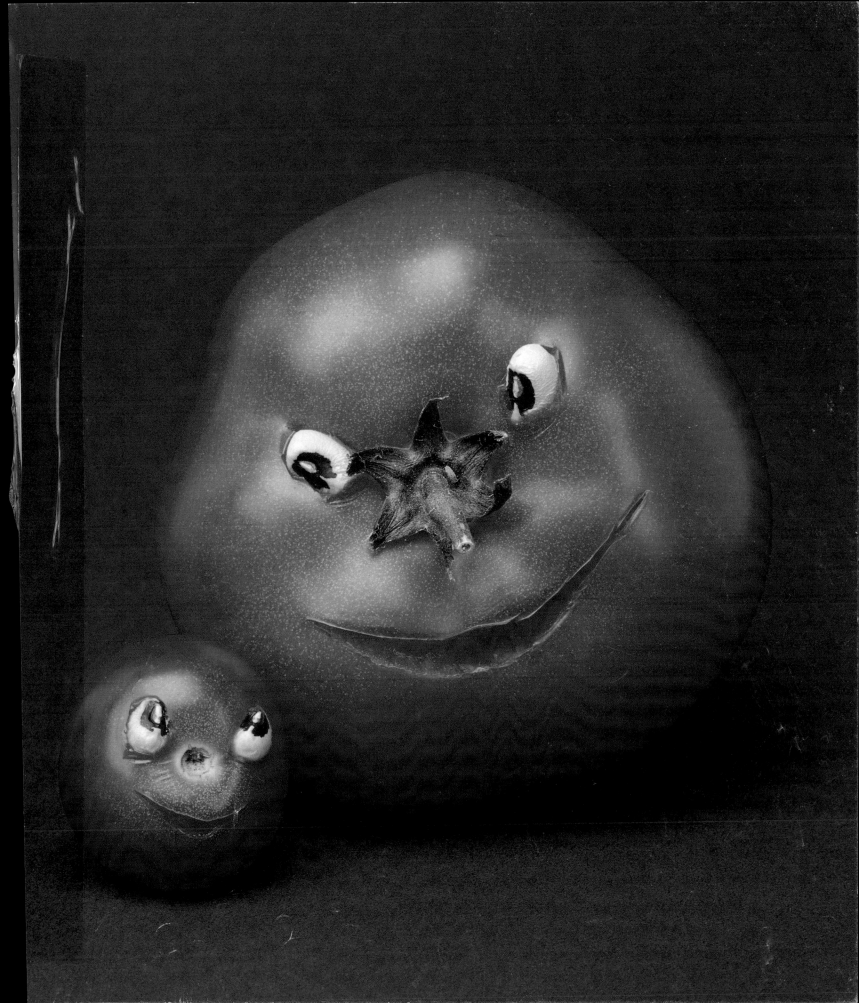

Disappointed too? When you are hurt, who comforts you?

So many smiles!
Can you decide
who's feeling safe?
Who's feeling pride?

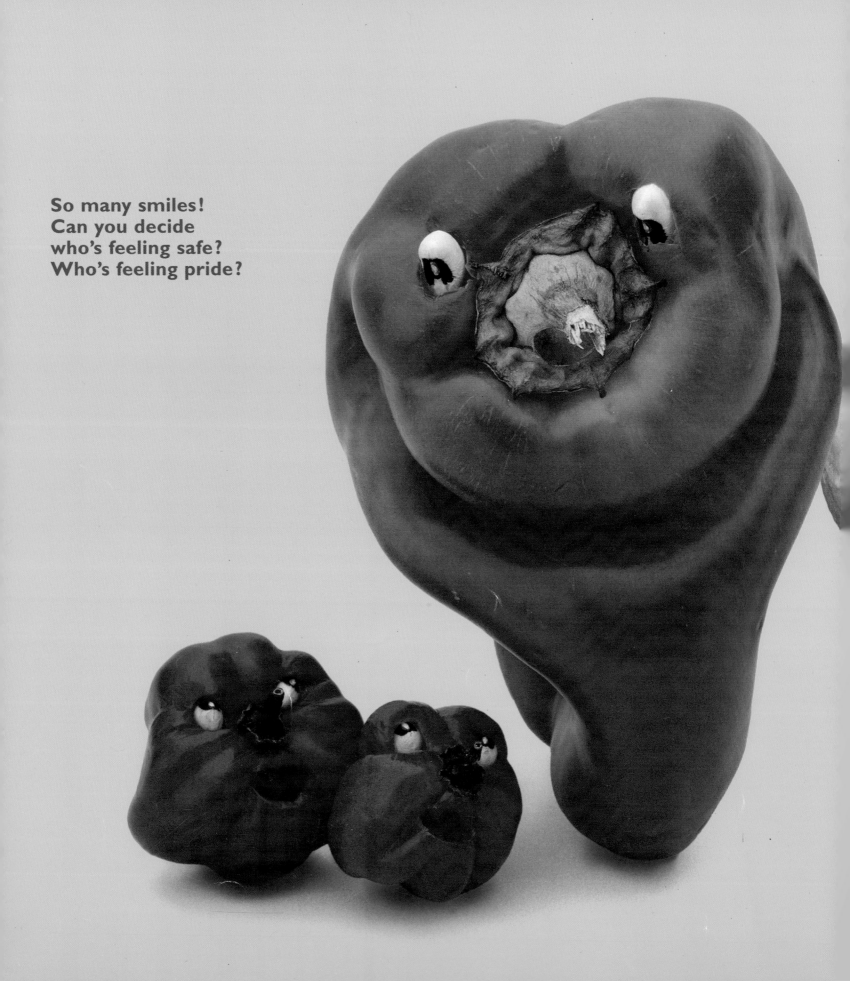

**Wired? Tired? Need a kiss?
Do you know anyone like this?**

Do you let your feelings show?
Who do you love? How do they know?

When how you feel is understood,
you have a friend, and that feels good.

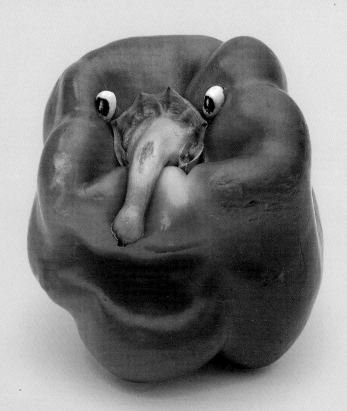

YOU FEELING?

For Mia, Eyck, Finn, and Elodie,
with love beyond words and vegetables
S.F.

For Oekie and in memory of Arie Jansma.
Early on the Jansma family showed me
the world of play.
J.E.

A NOTE ABOUT THE ART

To create these sculptures, markets throughout the New York metro-politan area were plumbed for expressive produce. These were carved using a simple Exacto knife and enhanced with other natural materials, such as black-eyed peas (for eyes) and beet-juice coloring (for mouths). The sculptures were then photographed against plain and colored backgrounds to achieve the desired effect and mood.

Book design by Erik Thé
Photography by Nimkin/Parrinello

Library of Congress Cataloging-in-Publication Data Available
ISBN 0-439-10431-9

10 9 8 7 6 5 4 3 2 1   9/9 0/0 01 02 03 04

Printed in the U.S.A. 37
First edition, October 1999

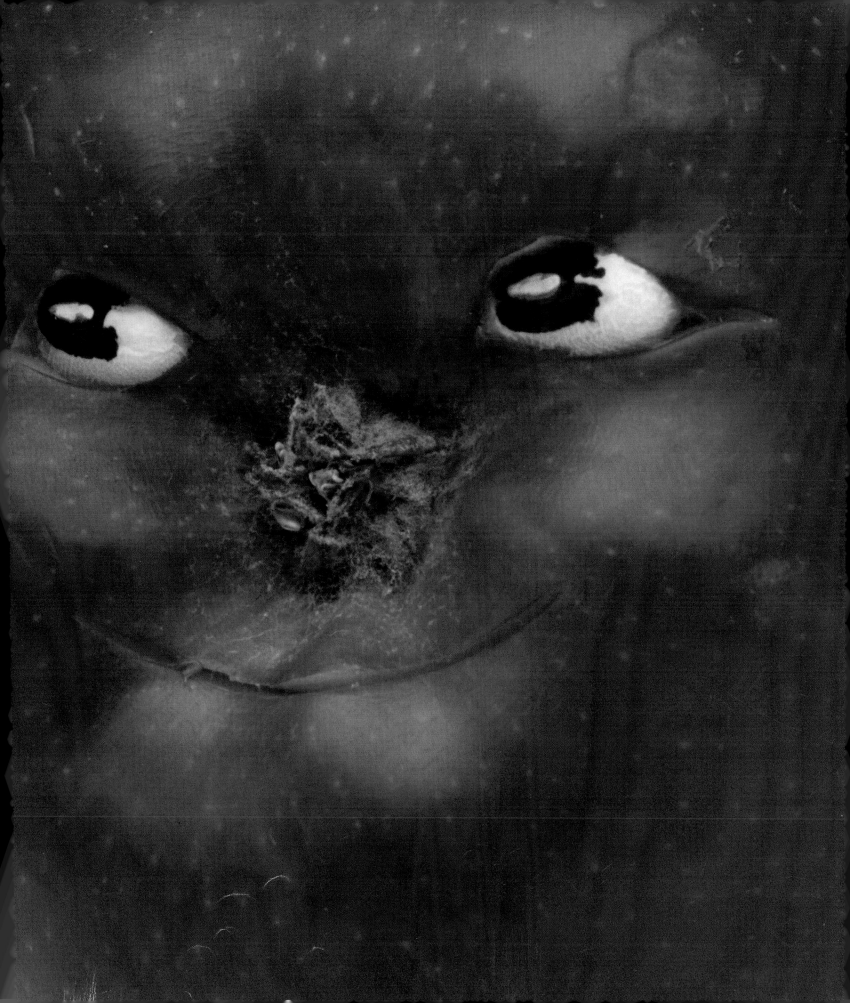